The Pug Who Wanted to Be a Unicorn

Also by Bella Swift

The Pug Who Wanted to Be a Reindeer

The Pug

Who Wanted to Be a

Unicorn

BY Bella Swift

ALADDIN New York London Toronto Sydney New Delhi

With special thanks to Anne Marie Ryan,
Nina Jones, and Artful Doodlers

ALADDIN
An imprint of Simon & Schuster Children's Publishing Division
1230 Avenue of the Americas, New York, New York 10020
First Aladdin paperback edition August 2021
Text copyright © 2018 by Orchard Books
Originally published in Great Britain in 2018 by the Watts Publishing Group.
Illustrations copyright © 2018 by Orchard Books
Also available in an Aladdin hardcover edition.
All rights reserved, including the right of reproduction in whole or in part in any form.
ALADDIN and related logo are registered trademarks of Simon & Schuster, Inc.
For information about special discounts for bulk purchases, please contact Simon & Schuster
Special Sales at 1-866-506-1949 or business@simonandschuster.com.
The Simon & Schuster Speakers Bureau can bring authors to your live event.
For more information or to book an event contact the Simon & Schuster Speakers Bureau
at 1-866-248-3049 or visit our website at www.simonspeakers.com.
The text of this book was set in Bembo Std.
Manufactured in the United States of America 0721 OFF
2 4 6 8 10 9 7 5 3 1
Library of Congress Control Number 2020949486
ISBN 9781534486799 (hc)
ISBN 9781534486782 (pbk)
ISBN 9781534486805 (ebook)

Contents

Prologue

Peggy wriggled her little bottom and snuggled closer to her two brothers and two sisters. The five little pug puppies were curled up against their mother's side, snoozing in a furry heap of paws and curly tails. Sighing dreamily, Peggy nuzzled her squashed black nose against her mum's soft, tan-colored fur.

Suddenly, her mum stood up, nudging the dozing puppies awake with her nose.

"Hey!" yelped Peggy's brother Pablo. "I was sleeping."

Yawning, the puppies clambered to their feet.

"Today's a very important day for all of you," announced their mum, gazing down at the puppies fondly with big brown eyes. "You're going home."

"Aren't we already home?" asked Peggy, puzzled.

"You're twelve weeks old now," her

mum said gently. "So your new owners are coming today. They are taking you to your forever homes."

Peggy stared at her mum in confusion, her wrinkled forehead creasing even more. *Forever home? What's that?*

"Don't worry, little ones," the puppies'

mum reassured them. "For every dog, there is a perfect owner. I know you will all find yours and be happy in your forever homes."

SLURP! SLURP! SLURP!

A rough pink tongue licked Peggy's face clean.

"Muuuuum!" protested Peggy, trying to squirm away from her mother's sloppy kisses.

"Don't wriggle," said her mother. "I

want you to look your best." After one final slurp, she moved on to wash Peggy's sister Polly.

When all the puppies' fur was clean, their mum looked at them proudly. "There! Now you're ready to meet your new owners."

"I hope my owner has a big garden," yipped Peggy's brother Paddy, panting with excitement.

"I hope my owner gives me lots of tasty treats," yapped Pippa, the greediest puppy of the litter.

"I hope my owner likes to take naps," said Pablo, yawning. He stretched out his front paws, sticking his bottom in the air.

"What about you, Peggy?" asked her mum gently. "What type of owner do you want?"

Peggy thought for a moment. A garden would be nice. So would tasty snacks. But that wasn't what Peggy wanted most of all. At last she said, "I hope my owner loves me."

Peggy's mum gazed at her puppies tenderly, her eyes shining with affection. "That's what I want for all of you, my dears."

Chapter One

CLICK!

Peggy's floppy black ears perked up as she heard the key turning in the lock. It could only mean one thing—her owner was back!

"She's home!" Peggy cried, scampering around the smoky-gray cat who was basking in a patch of sunlight on the floor. She batted the cat's nose with her paw. "Wake up, Misha. She's back!"

The cat opened her eyes slightly, revealing two green slivers. "Big deal," Misha hissed, swiping at Peggy with her sharp claws.

Oops, thought Peggy. Even though she had lived with the cat and her owner, Suzanne, for two months, she always forgot how grumpy Misha was when she woke up. Or anytime. Unlike Peggy, the cat didn't seem to mind being left on her own for hours.

"Last one to the door's a rotten egg,"

cried Peggy. She rushed to the front door, her claws skittering on the polished floorboards.

WHEE! Her paws slipped out from under her and she slid on her bottom.

WHUMP! Peggy crashed into the front door just as a lady in an elegant designer outfit pushed it open. As her owner dropped bulging shopping bags on the floor, Peggy scrambled back to her paws.

"Hello!" Peggy barked, trying to get Suzanne's attention. "Do you want to play?" Peggy ran around and around her owner's legs in circles until she started to feel dizzy.

"Hi, darling!" the lady said into the phone pressed to her ear. "I'll meet you there in half an hour."

Ooh! thought Peggy. It sounded like they were going out!

Peggy loved going for walks. Well, they weren't really walks. Most of the time she rode in Suzanne's handbag. Peggy wished she could walk too, but her short little legs couldn't keep up with her owner's long strides. But at least she could peek out from the bag and see the world around her—birds flying through the air, cars whooshing past, children zooming by on scooters.

"Can we go out now?" Peggy begged. "Please, please, pretty please with sausages on top."

Misha padded into the hallway, her tail twitching. "When will you get it through that wrinkly head of yours, runt?" she said. "Humans can't understand a word you're saying."

Peggy ignored the cat. She barked louder, pawing at Suzanne's legs.

"Be quiet, Peggy," Suzanne said, pressing her fingers to her temples. "All that yapping is giving me a headache."

Purring softly, Misha rubbed against her owner's legs. The cat shot Peggy a triumphant look as Suzanne bent down to stroke her.

Peggy whined sadly, and Suzanne patted her head briskly. Peggy's damp black nose tickled as she caught a whiff of her owner's flowery perfume.

ACHOO! ACHOOOO!

Peggy sneezed, spraying doggie dribble all over her owner's shoes. *Oopsie!*

"Ew," said Misha, her whiskers twitching.

"Dogs are so gross." She licked her paws and began to wash herself neatly.

"Ugh," said Suzanne. "I'd better go and get changed." She marched into the bedroom and dumped her shopping bags on the floor. Peggy followed her in and noticed something interesting sticking out from under the bed. She pounced on the high-heeled shoe and began to chew, the leather squeaking against her teeth.

"Hey!" cried Suzanne, grabbing the shoe and pulling hard.

Yay! thought Peggy. *Tug-of-war!*

Chomping down on the shoe, Peggy pulled as hard as she could. But Suzanne

was stronger than she was. Her owner yanked so hard that Peggy let go of the shoe. Suzanne flew backward and landed on top of her shopping bags.

"You win!" barked Peggy, licking her owner's face to congratulate her.

"Those are my favorite shoes!" Suzanne cried, pushing Peggy away.

"Mine too!" barked Peggy. It was so nice to have something in common with her owner!

Standing up, Suzanne seized her handbag and headed for the door.

"Wait!" barked Peggy, chasing after her owner. "Don't forget me!"

SLAM!

The door shut and Peggy was alone. Again. Well, apart from Misha.

"Will you play with me, Misha?" Peggy asked the cat hopefully.

"As if," said Misha, curling up on a cushion and shutting her eyes.

Peggy sighed. She knew she was a lucky

dog. She had a dog bed with velvet pillows. She had a different sparkly collar for every day of the week. Her dinners were served in a shiny gold bowl. But her owner was always too busy to play. Sometimes Peggy really missed her brothers and sisters.

Resting her paws on the back of the white sofa, Peggy pressed her nose against

the window and gazed out at the winter sunshine. She saw a friendly-looking dog snuffling around in the garden next door. "Hey!" she barked. "Do you want to play?" But the dog couldn't hear her through the glass.

"Fine," Peggy told herself. "I'll just have to entertain myself."

She wandered into the kitchen and nibbled some of her food. There was a pile of newspapers on the floor next to her bowl. The one on top had a picture of a jolly-looking man with a big white beard. He was wearing a bright red suit and looked very kind. *I bet he likes to play*, thought Peggy.

Nudging the stack with her nose, she tipped it over, spreading newspapers all over the kitchen floor. Turning the pages with her paws, Peggy looked at the pictures. She liked the ones of animals best of all!

A voice snarled, "Hey! A little privacy, please!"

Startled, Peggy looked up from the newspaper. Misha was standing in her litter box on the other side of the kitchen. The cat glared at her.

"Sorry!" Peggy yelped. Embarrassed, she bolted from the kitchen, tripping over her water bowl on the way out. *SPLASH!*

Water spilled everywhere, drenching Peggy. She ran down the hallway, leaving a trail of wet pawprints behind her.

I'd better dry myself off, Peggy thought.

She shook herself, spraying drops of water all over the living room. Then she rolled around and around on the sofa, drying her fur on the fluffy cushions. It felt a bit like rolling around with her brothers and sisters.

Peggy pounced on a cushion, wrestling with it the way she used to play-fight with Paddy and Pippa. "Grrrr," she growled, sinking her teeth into the soft cushion.

RIIIIPPPP! The cushion tore open, scattering white feathers into the air. Peggy

jumped off the sofa, trying to catch feathers in her paws. She missed the feathers, but knocked over a vase.

CRASH! The vase smashed on the floor, scattering glass everywhere.

Oopsie! Not wanting to cut her paws on the

glass, Peggy scrambled back onto the sofa, her bottom resting on the remote control.

CLICK! The television switched on. The most gorgeous creature Peggy had ever seen filled the screen—a white horse with a glowing, rainbow-striped horn and a flowing, glittery mane. As it soared through the sky, fluttering its colorful wings, a song blasted out of the TV:

I'm Sparkalina the magical unicorn,
Granting wishes with my rainbow horn!
Always be yourself, whoever you may be,
Unless you can be a unicorn like
MEEEEEEE!

Her eyes wide, Peggy watched the show, transfixed. Sparkalina was amazing! Her magic horn could make flowers grow, turn clouds to cotton candy, and draw rainbows in the sky!

When the show was over, Peggy settled down on a soft cushion. *Sparkalina's so cool,* she thought, as her eyes began to close. Then the little pug fell fast asleep, dreaming of beautiful unicorns flying through the sky.

Chapter Two

"NOOOOOO!"

A piercing shriek woke Peggy up. Suzanne was standing in the living room, a horrified look on her face. Feathers, shards of glass, and scraps of newspaper were strewn all over the floor. Tan-colored dog hair and mucky pawprints were scattered all over the white sofa.

"I told her a dog would be nothing but trouble," purred Misha as she wound her sleek body around Suzanne's legs.

Peggy gulped. The apartment *did* look a bit messy. "I was going to tidy up . . . ," she barked apologetically. "I was just having a nap first."

"That's it!" said Suzanne, stuffing Peggy into her handbag. She didn't even check whether the bag matched Peggy's collar.

Peggy's heart leaped with excitement. Finally, they were going out!

As Suzanne strode out of the apartment,

Peggy popped her head out of the handbag. Her floppy ears fluttered in the chilly
winter air as her owner marched along
briskly. Peggy really hoped they were going

to the park. Suzanne
had taken her a few
times, and there had
been loads of lovely
things to sniff—piles
of leaves, scurrying
squirrels, and other
dogs' bottoms.

But Suzanne went
past the park with-
out stopping. *I wonder*

where she's taking me? Peggy thought.

Eventually, Suzanne came to a halt in front of a big building. The sound of barking was coming from inside. *Ooh!* thought Peggy. It sounded like there were other dogs to play with! Her tail wagged excitedly. She couldn't wait to meet some new friends.

Inside, the barking got even louder.

"Hello," said an older lady wearing a sweater with a snowman on it. "Welcome to Doldrum's Dog Home. I'm Doreen. Can I help you?"

"Yes," said Suzanne, plonking her handbag down. "You can take my dog."

Doreen frowned. "What do you mean?"

"I'm sick of her chewing my shoes and making a mess," said Suzanne, scooping Peggy out of the bag and thrusting her at Doreen. "I don't want her anymore."

Hang on a minute, thought Peggy, struggling to wriggle out of Doreen's arms. *What's going on?*

"Please reconsider," pleaded Doreen. "Puppies are a handful, but they do settle down eventually."

"She's right!" Peggy barked. "I'll settle down! I'll be good! I promise!"

"Nope," said Suzanne, picking up her handbag. "I'm done with dogs. I'm sticking to cats from now on—they're so much easier."

"But our shelter is full up," protested Doreen. "I really don't have space for another dog—not even a little one."

"NOOOO!" howled Peggy. "Don't leave me here!"

"Sorry," said Suzanne, turning to leave. "Not my problem."

"Where am I supposed to put her?" Doreen called after her.

But it was no use. Suzanne was gone.

"Oh dear," said Doreen, sighing. "Some people think that pugs are just fashion accessories." She squinted at the tag on Peggy's collar. "Nice to meet you, Peggy. Let's take you outside to meet the others."

She led Peggy to a big grassy area surrounded by a fence. Peggy's eyes widened. She'd never seen so many dogs in one place! A sleek greyhound sprinted around the pen—a blur of gray—while a tubby bulldog snored noisily in the winter sunshine. A tiny terrier was wrestling with a shaggy sheepdog (and seemed to be winning), while a mastiff chewed on a tatty soccer ball. The noise of all the barking made Peggy's ears hurt.

"Don't worry, Peggy," said Doreen, setting her down inside the pen. "We'll find you a nice new home soon, I promise." She unfurled a hose and started filling up water bowls.

"Ha!" grunted an old basset hound, hobbling over to give Peggy a curious sniff. "Don't be so sure about that."

"Why? How long have you been here?" Peggy asked.

"Five years," said the basset hound.

"You mean in dog years?" asked Peggy hopefully.

The older dog laughed ruefully and shook her head. "Hey, everyone!" she barked. "We've got a newcomer."

Peggy trembled as a pack of dogs crowded round to get a closer look.

"Aww!" said a scruffy mutt with a cone around his neck. "She's just a puppy!"

"Great," sniffed a haughty-looking poodle.

"That's all we need around here. More competition."

"There's been a big mistake," said Peggy. "I already have a home. My owner will be back to get me soon."

"That's what we all thought, dearie," said a golden retriever with kind eyes.

Peggy's eyes filled with tears and she started to howl.

"Now, now," said the old basset hound. "Crying won't solve anything. Run along and play." She lay down on the ground and began to snore loudly.

Peggy cheered up a bit. It was true that she'd wanted someone to play with. Well, there were plenty of potential playmates here! She wandered over to the mastiff with the ball. "Can I play too?" she asked politely.

"Get lost," snapped the big dog.

Peggy found a rubber chicken and started chewing on it.

"Hey!" snarled a Staffie, baring his sharp teeth. "That's mine!" He snatched the toy away from Peggy.

Peggy rested her head on her front paws. *Why doesn't anyone want to play?* Was she going to have to live here with these unfriendly dogs forever? Her mum had said that every dog had a perfect owner. "Where's mine?" she whimpered.

That night, Peggy had to share a pen with the elderly basset hound, who was called Mavis.

"Here you go, Peggy," said Doreen, spreading a blanket on the concrete floor. "This will have to do." Then she shut the door of the pen, locking the two dogs in.

"I'm too old for a roommate," Mavis grumbled. But she budged over to make space for Peggy.

Peggy lay on the hard floor, trying to get comfortable. Her tummy rumbled. The mean mastiff had gobbled up her dinner before she'd even taken a bite.

As Peggy tossed and turned, Mavis began

to snore loudly, making the whole pen shake.

ZZZzzzz!

Whenever Peggy's eyes started to close, a dog would bark, startling her awake  again. She shivered in the dark, missing her velvet dog bed, until sunrise.

"Good morning," Mavis said, yawning. "I slept like a puppy—how about you?"

"I didn't sleep a wink," said Peggy.

"You'll soon get used to the noise," said Mavis. She chuckled. "Of course it helps if you're a bit deaf like me."

After breakfast, Doreen took the dogs outside. Suddenly, a family came into the outdoor area. The dad was holding a big dog bed, the mum was pushing a little girl in a stroller, a teenage boy was wearing headphones, and an older girl was wearing a T-shirt with a

unicorn it. Peggy gasped. It was Sparkalina—
the unicorn from the TV show!

"Quick!" said Mavis. "Places, everyone!
Remember—look sad!"

The dogs all hurried over to the fence.
Some whimpered mournfully, while others rested their heads on their front paws.
The mastiff started limping, even though a
moment before, he'd been walking fine on
all four paws. Mavis's droopy eyes looked
even sadder than usual.

"What's everyone doing?" Peggy whispered.

"Trying to make these people feel sorry
for us," the golden retriever said.

"Why?" asked Peggy.

"So they adopt us, dummy," said the poodle, fluffing up her poofy tail.

Doreen put down a bag of kibble and hurried over to greet the family.

"Hello," said the mum. "There was nobody at reception so we came out here. We wanted to donate this dog bed to the shelter. It belonged to our old dog, Baxter, who died not long ago."

"I'm so sorry to hear that," said Doreen, taking the bed. "It's very hard to lose a much-loved pet. Have you thought about adopting another dog?"

"I'm not sure we're ready for that yet," said the mum.

"Me look at doggies!" cried the little girl in the stroller.

The family peered through the fence, and dogs clamored around them.

"That one's almost as big as Baxter was," said the boy, pointing to the mastiff. The big dog growled menacingly.

"But Baxter was gentle," said the girl in the unicorn T-shirt, her eyes filling with tears.

She really misses Baxter, thought Peggy. She stuck her nose through a gap in the fence and licked the girl's hand, trying to cheer her up.

"That tickles," the girl said, giggling. She

stroked Peggy's head through the fence. Peggy was happy to see her smiling.

"Would you consider fostering a dog?" asked Doreen. "We're full to capacity at the moment. We don't even have space for little Peggy here."

"Hmm. Maybe that's not a bad idea," said the dad. "It might help us decide whether we're ready for another dog."

"If you took Peggy home over Christmas, it would really help us out," said the lady. "You're experienced dog owners, and she seems to have bonded with your daughter already."

"What do you think, kids?" asked the mum. "Ruby?"

The little girl in the stroller kicked her legs and squealed, "Doggie!"

"What about you, Chloe?"

The girl in the unicorn T-shirt nodded.

"Finn?" asked the mum.

The teenage boy frowned. "Pugs are too small. They aren't proper dogs."

"But she's so cute," said his sister Chloe.

Please say yes, thought Peggy.

Eventually, the boy shrugged. "I guess it's okay—if it's only for Christmas."

Yippee! thought Peggy, her corkscrew tail waggling.

"This is your big chance," said Mavis. "Don't mess it up."

"I won't!" barked Peggy.

She had a new home for Christmas. And if she was a very good dog, maybe she'd be able to stay forever!

Chapter Three

"Welcome to our home, Peggy," said Mum, setting Peggy down in the hallway.

Peggy took a few steps forward and sniffed the air. Suzanne's apartment had smelled of flowery perfume, cleaning fluid, and kitty litter. This house smelled like muddy sneakers, homemade soup, and crayons. *Perfect!* thought Peggy, inhaling deeply. It smelled exactly like a home should smell.

It's not your home yet, she reminded herself. *It's just for Christmas.* She knew that if this family decided that they didn't like her, she'd be going straight back to the dog shelter.

"Right, we'd better get dinner started," Dad said.

"Can we have spaghetti tonight?" asked Finn.

"If you kids help," said Mum.

The children followed their parents into the kitchen. Ruby sat in her high chair,

coloring, while the two older children set about chopping vegetables. As Mum made a salad, Dad stirred a pot on the stove. Soon, the house started to smell even more delicious. Peggy sat on the kitchen floor, licking her lips as she watched them cook.

"Don't forget to add these, Dad!" said Chloe. She carried a chopping board over to her father and—*WHOOPS!*—tripped over Peggy. Sliced carrots spilled all over the floor.

CRUNCH! CRUNCH! CRUNCH! As quick as a flash, Peggy gobbled up the pieces of carrot.

"Thanks for cleaning up, Peggy," said

Dad, chuckling. "I can see you're going to be a big help around here."

"Look, kids," said Mum, laughing. "Peggy's setting a good example by eating up her vegetables."

Finn made a face. "That's about all she's good for."

Mum opened the refrigerator and took out a carton of milk. "Remember the time we had a picnic and Baxter ate all the sandwiches?"

"And when Baxter ate my whole birthday cake and we had to take him to the vet?" said Chloe.

"Baxter was awesome," said Finn. He

looked down at Peggy, unimpressed. "Big dogs are way more fun than little dogs."

"Ignore him," Chloe told Peggy. "Little dogs are fun, too."

Baxter was lucky to have had a family who loved him so much, thought Peggy. She gazed at the pictures stuck on the refrigerator. Baxter was in almost all of them. One

showed Finn hugging an enormous St. Bernard. Another picture showed Chloe as a toddler, riding the huge dog like a horse. There was one of Ruby as a baby, napping on a blanket next to Baxter.

Peggy wondered if they could ever love another dog as much as they had loved Baxter. Suddenly, she felt sad.

"Dinner's ready!" announced Dad, carrying a big bowl of spaghetti to the table.

"What's Peggy going to eat?" asked Chloe.

"I cooked some hamburger for her," said Mum. She set down an enormous dog bowl filled with tasty meat. Peggy ran over and started gobbling it up.

"We'll need to get her a new bowl," said Chloe, giggling. "Baxter's old one is too big for her."

"We can pick one up when we go shopping tomorrow," said Mum.

"Are we getting our Christmas tree?" asked Chloe.

"Yes," said Dad. "And maybe we can visit Santa Claus, too."

"Santa!" cried Ruby, banging her spoon on her tray.

"I've still got some Christmas gifts to buy," said Finn.

"Are you getting one for your girl-friend?" Chloe teased Finn.

"Jasmine's NOT my girlfriend," Finn said, his cheeks turning red. "She's just the singer in my band." He flicked a forkful of spaghetti at his sister, but it missed and landed on Peggy's head.

Chloe giggled. "It looks like Peggy's wearing a wig."

Everyone laughed—except Finn.

SLURP! The spaghetti slid off Peggy's head and into her mouth. There was a little bathtub in the kitchen so Peggy waded in to clean herself off. She paddled about in the water, splashing it everywhere.

"Peggy's having a bath!" said Chloe, smiling.

"In Baxter's water bowl!" Dad chuckled.

"Silly doggie!" laughed Ruby.

Finn just rolled his eyes.

"I guess we need to get her a new water bowl, too," said Chloe.

"Speaking of baths . . . ," said Mum, giving Ruby's sauce-smeared face a wipe with a napkin. "Let's get you cleaned up."

Mum carried Ruby upstairs, followed by Finn, who said he wanted to work on a new song.

"Where's Peggy going to sleep tonight?" asked Chloe as she helped her father clear the table.

"We should let her decide," said Dad.

"Come on," Chloe said, picking Peggy up. "Let's give you the grand tour." She carried Peggy upstairs and set her down on the landing. Peggy peeked into a room with posters of rock bands plastered on the walls and piles of dirty clothes scattered all over the floor.

"Who said you and that mutt could come into my room?" demanded Finn, glaring at Chloe and Peggy.

"I'm just showing Peggy around," Chloe said. She wrinkled her nose. "Not that she'd want to sleep in your stinky old room."

"Baxter liked it in here," said Finn, scowling.

Peggy sniffed at the clothes on the floor, wondering if they might make a cozy bed. There was even a half-eaten pizza under the bed! *Perfect for a midnight snack*, thought Peggy.

She saw a wooden stick on the floor and started chewing it.

"Oi! That's my drumstick!" said Finn, snatching it away from Peggy. Then—

BOOM! CRASH! BOOM!

He started pounding on a drum kit.

Maybe not! thought Peggy, her ears ring-ing. She darted out of Finn's bedroom. She was pretty sure he didn't want her sleeping in his room, anyway.

Ah! Peggy thought, going into the next room along. This was much better. There were toys everywhere—hard, plastic ones and soft, cuddly ones. All just perfect for a puppy to chew on! Peggy started to gnaw on a teddy bear. But then—

"Peggy!" shrieked Ruby, running into her bedroom in her pajamas. The toddler picked Peggy up and squeezed her so tight, she could barely breathe.

Yikes, thought Peggy,

wriggling free of Ruby's grasp. *She thinks I'm a cuddly toy.*

"And this is my room," said Chloe, opening the next door along.

Wow! thought Peggy, gazing around in awe. The lamp had a Sparkalina lampshade. The walls were covered with pictures of flying unicorns. And there was a fluffy rug right by a bed with a bright pink Sparkalina duvet cover.

"Story?" asked Ruby, toddling into her sister's room holding a picture book.

"Okay," said Chloe. She and Ruby snuggled up together. "Come and join us, Peggy," called Chloe, patting the bed.

Really? thought Peggy, amazed. Suzanne had never let Peggy on her bed. She didn't want to get dog hair on her expensive sheets.

Peggy climbed up onto the bed and squeezed in between the two girls. Chloe opened the book and began to read a story about Sparkalina while Ruby stroked Peggy's back. Peggy hadn't felt this comfy since she'd left her mum.

"'You can be anything you want to be,'" read Chloe, "'as long as you believe in yourself.'" She shut the book. "'The end.'"

"Me want a noonicorn," said Ruby, yawning and rubbing her eyes sleepily.

"Me too," said Chloe, kissing her little

sister's head. "That would be so amazing."

Oh dear, thought Peggy sadly. It wasn't just Finn who didn't want Peggy for a pet. The girls didn't want a pug, either. They wanted a unicorn!

Suddenly, she remembered what Sparka-lina had said in the story. *I can be anything I want to be*, thought Peggy, *so I'll be a unicorn!*

If she could find a way to become like Sparkalina, she could stay with Chloe and her family forever!

Chapter Four

"Walkies, Peggy!" called Chloe the next morning, holding up a lead.

Peggy hung back, eyeing the lead suspiciously. She didn't want to get her hopes up. The last time she'd thought she was going on a walk, she had ended up at the dog shelter!

But Chloe smiled and clipped on the lead. "It will be fun. We're going shopping."

Mum buckled Ruby into her stroller. Then the family headed out, bundled up in coats, scarves, and woolly hats. The winter air was crisp, but Peggy's fur kept her toasty warm as she trotted obediently at Chloe's heel.

In the town center, the sidewalks were crowded with people doing their Christmas shopping. Big, clompy feet hurried past Peggy, narrowly missing her little paws. Frightened, Peggy huddled close to Chloe's legs. She didn't want to get trodden on!

"Peggy's scared," said Chloe.
She picked Peggy up and
plopped her onto her
little sister's lap.

This is more like it!
thought Peggy as
she sat on Ruby's
lap, watching the
crowds of shop-
pers whizz past.

"Let's go in here
first," said Mum, entering
the pet shop.

Cool! thought Peggy, gazing long-
ingly at the shelves of squeaky toys and

tasty-looking bones. The shop sold everything a pet owner could possibly need—
from birdseed and bones, to brushes and beds.

While Mum chose packets of dog food,
Chloe held up a small red food bowl and a
matching water bowl. "What do you think,
Peggy?"

Peggy wagged her curly tail. They were
just the right size for her!

"We've got to get this," said Chloe, holding up a squeaky toy shaped like a turkey
leg.

"Why?" asked Mum.

"Because it's a *drum*stick," said Chloe.
"Get it?"

The rest of the family groaned at Chloe's cheesy joke, but Mum popped the toy into the basket.

Peggy felt so happy, she thought her heart might burst. It was so nice to feel like part of a family. *I could get used to this. . . .*

When they stepped out of the pet shop, Chloe pointed to the clothing store across the street. A girl with long, dark hair was coming out of it, holding a shopping bag. "Look, Finn," said Chloe. "It's Jasmine."

"Stop pointing," hissed Finn, his cheeks flushing with embarrassment.

"Finn has a crush on Jasmine," Chloe whispered loudly.

"No, I don't!" said Finn, turning even redder.

The girl caught sight of them and waved. She crossed the street to join them.

"Is this your dog?" she asked Finn.

"No," said Finn. "I mean, sort of. Just for Christmas."

"OMG," cooed Jasmine. She crouched down to stroke Peggy. "She's, like, the cutest thing I've ever seen."

Peggy licked Jasmine's face. She could see why Finn liked her.

"I guess so," said Finn, shrugging. "If you like little dogs with squashed faces."

Finn and Jasmine went to get hot chocolates, and Dad rushed off to buy some Christmas tree lights.

"I'm just going to buy some wrapping paper," Mum told Chloe. "You wait here with Ruby and Peggy."

Chloe pushed the stroller to the toyshop window. Peggy's eyes widened as she saw the display. It was full of Sparkalina toys! There was a unicorn with wings that really flapped, Sparkalina's pink plastic play stable, and a styling head with a horn that lit up and a long, glittery mane to plait.

"Noonicorns!" cried Ruby.

Wow, thought Peggy, pressing her damp black nose against the window.

"I want one exactly like that," said Chloe, pointing to the toy with wings.

A television screen inside the shop was playing an advertisement. A little girl sang a jingle as she brushed a Sparkalina toy's tail:

I can brush her mane and braid her hair,

Flap her wings and she flies through the air.

Her magic horn really glows with light,

Never has a unicorn shone so bright!

No wonder Chloe wants a unicorn, thought Peggy. Unicorns could fly and do magic. Pugs couldn't do anything cool like that.

Mum hurried back holding several rolls

of wrapping paper. "Shall we go and see Santa Claus now?" she said. "The line's not too long."

Chloe wheeled her little sister—and Peggy—to Santa's place. It was a wooden hut in the middle of the shopping center, decorated with sparkly fake snow. Inside it, a man with a white beard and a red suit sat on a big armchair with a sack of toys next to him. Peggy recognized him instantly.

"That's the man from the newspaper!" she barked excitedly.

"Aw," said Chloe. "Peggy wants to visit Santa, too."

First Ruby went to see Santa, holding

her mum's hand. She came back grinning and clutching a gingerbread man. When it was Chloe's turn, she picked Peggy up and went inside the hut.

"Ho, ho, ho!" chuckled Santa. "Have you been good this year?"

"Yes," said Chloe. "Well, mostly."

"And what do you want for Christmas?" Santa asked her.

"A unicorn with wings that can fly," said Chloe. "And . . ." She hesitated, then whispered something into Santa's ear.

"And what do you want, little doggie?" asked Santa, smiling.

"I want to be a unicorn with wings," barked

Peggy. "So I can stay with Chloe forever."

"I think the puppy wants a bone," said Santa, patting Peggy on the head.

"No!" yelped Peggy. "That's not what I said!"

"Happy Christmas," said Santa, giving Chloe a gingerbread man.

"Can we get our Christmas tree now?" Chloe asked her mum when they were back outside.

Leaving the shopping center, they walked to a place selling Christmas trees and wreaths. Dad and Finn were waiting for them there.

"Out!" cried Ruby, kicking her legs.

Mum unclipped the harness and let Ruby out of the stroller.

Peggy sniffed the pine-scented air. It smelled just like being in the woods! There were rows and rows of trees, but no one could decide which one was best.

"I want this one," said Finn, pointing to an enormous tree.

"Too tall," said Mum, shaking her head. "Our ceilings aren't high enough."

"This one's pretty," said Chloe.

"Hmm," said Dad, scratching his chin. "I think the trunk is a bit crooked."

"Which one do you like, Ruby?" asked Mum. There was no answer. "Ruby!"

Mum called, looking around in alarm.

Ruby had vanished!

Mum and Dad sprinted off in opposite directions. Finn crawled around on the ground, searching for Ruby under the trees. Chloe dropped Peggy's lead and ran off, calling her sister's name.

Nobody noticed the trail of gingerbread crumbs on the ground. Nobody, that is, except for Peggy. . . .

Gobbling up the tasty crumbs, Peggy followed the trail until she found Ruby. The little girl was happily munching her gingerbread man under a Christmas tree.

WOOF! WOOF! WOOF!

Peggy barked as loud as she could to alert the others.

Everyone ran over. "Oh my goodness," Mum gasped, hugging Ruby. "You gave us all such a fright."

"You mustn't wander off like that," Dad scolded her.

"Peggy's a star!" said Chloe, picking her up.

"I wouldn't go that far," said Finn. "But at least she found us a Christmas tree."

Everyone looked at the tree Ruby had been sitting underneath. It was tall, but not too tall. It was straight and full, its pine needles glossy and dark green.

"It's perfect," said Mum, smiling.

"Just like you!" said Chloe, kissing the top of Peggy's head.

They paid for the Christmas tree at a little wooden hut, and a man wrapped it up in plastic netting. Then Dad and Finn hoisted the tree onto their shoulders.

"Me help too!" cried Ruby.

"You can help by holding Peggy," said Mum, buckling Ruby into her stroller.

Chloe carefully placed Peggy on her little sister's lap, and they began to walk home for lunch.

Dad started whistling a Christmas carol, and soon the whole family was singing along. Peggy let out a happy yip.

"Peggy's singing, too!" said Chloe, grinning.

Peggy gazed up at her new friend adoringly. *This has been the best walk ever!*

Chapter Five

"A bit to the left!" called Mum, as Dad and Finn adjusted the Christmas tree in its base. The fresh, clean scent of pine filled the living room.

Peggy cocked her head to the side. She wasn't sure why they'd brought the tree inside, but humans were always doing strange things, like wearing clothes and using funny metal things to eat with.

"Over to the right a smidge," said Mum. Dad and Finn straightened the tree up, then stepped back to admire their work.

"Lovely!" declared Mum.

"Now for the best bit," said Chloe, open-ing a big cardboard box. "Decorating it!"

Peggy peered into the box. It was full of shiny things— sparkly silver garlands, glittery baubles, and a twinkly gold star.

As Mum and Dad wrapped fairy lights around the tree, the children hung decorations on the branches. There were wooden toy soldiers, little knitted stockings, and lacy snowflakes.

"I can't believe I was so tiny once!" said Chloe, holding up a clay ornament with a baby handprint pressed into it.

"It seems like just yesterday," said Dad, ruffling her hair affectionately.

"Here's the one Baxter made," said Finn, taking out an ornament with an enormous pawprint on it. "He was such a cool dog."

Chloe nodded as she hung her baby

handprint decoration on the tree.

"Noonicorn!" said Ruby, hanging a glass ornament shaped like a unicorn on a low branch.

"That's so pretty," said Chloe, stroking the unicorn's horn with her finger.

Peggy shook her head sadly. She'd never have her own ornament because she wasn't here for good. Finn didn't like her. And Chloe didn't want a boring little dog—she wanted a unicorn.

The children began to hang sparkly tinsel on the tree.

"Look at me!" Chloe said, laughing. She wrapped a length of silver tinsel garland around her neck like a boa and strutted around. "I'm a movie star!"

Peggy suddenly perked up. Chloe had just given her a great idea. Sparkalina had a glittery mane. Maybe she could have one, too!

Peggy poked a garland of tinsel with her nose, nudging it over her head so that it

hung down her back. She hoped it looked like a unicorn's flowing mane.

"Look at Peggy!" said Chloe. "She wants to be a movie star, too."

No, thought Peggy. *Not a movie star—a unicorn!* She sighed sadly. Her tinsel mane hadn't fooled anyone.

"You're already a star, Peggy," said Chloe, plucking the tinsel off her head and hanging it on the tree. "You found Ruby."

"Speaking of stars . . . ," said Mum. She stood on her tiptoes and put a gold star on the top of the tree. Then Dad flicked a switch and the fairy lights twinkled, changing color from red, to yellow, to blue, to green.

Peggy stared at the Christmas tree, astonished. The beautiful colored lights were glowing—just like Sparkalina's magic rainbow horn. Could the magic lights turn her into a unicorn? She had to find out!

Peggy bit the end of the lights and tugged. The Christmas tree teetered to the right. *Come on,* thought Peggy, giving the string of lights another sharp yank. The tree wobbled to the left.

"Whoa!" cried Finn.

Peggy gave one more pull and—

CRASH! The Christmas tree fell on top of her.

Am I a unicorn now? wondered Peggy,

crawling out from under the branches.

A shiny gold bauble rolled across the living room floor and landed by her front paws. Peggy peered down at it eagerly and saw . . . a pug tangled up in fairy lights.

"Oh, Peggy," said Mum, shaking her head in dismay. "What have you done?"

"How can such a tiny dog make such a big mess?" said Dad, looking cross.

Peggy closed her eyes and cowered, remembering how angry her last owner had been when she'd made a mess. Then she heard a noise. But it didn't sound like shouting. It sounded like . . . laughter.

Peggy opened her eyes.

"That was hilarious," hooted Finn. He took a picture of Peggy with his phone. "I'm going to send it to Jasmine." He blushed. "Only because she thinks pugs are cute."

"What were you trying to do?" Chloe asked Peggy, untangling the puppy's paws from the fairy lights.

I was just trying to become a unicorn, thought Peggy. *For you.*

The magic lights hadn't worked, but at least the family wasn't taking her back to the dog shelter. Yet. . . .

"I'd forgotten how much work puppies

are," sighed Dad, helping Mum re-right the Christmas tree.

"I know," said Mum. "It's like having two toddlers in the house."

Oh dear, thought Peggy. The grown-ups sounded really annoyed.

Everyone helped hang the ornaments back on the tree, and soon everything was back in order.

"Can I make some unicorn slime?" asked Chloe.

"Unicorn slime?" asked Mum, confused. "What on earth is that?"

"It's glittery slime," said Chloe. "Some-one at school gave me a recipe."

"Fine, as long as you tidy up when you're finished," said Mum.

"Me help too!" called Ruby.

In the kitchen, Peggy watched curiously as Chloe got out glue, baking soda, soap, and rainbow glitter. Chloe carefully measured out the ingredients and mixed them all together.

"Squishy," said Ruby, sticking her fingers into the gooey mixture.

"That's how it's supposed to be," said Chloe, shaking in some more glitter.

The girls played with the sparkly slime, stretching it out, rolling it into a ball, and molding it into different shapes.

"Look, Peggy!" said Chloe. "I made a unicorn." She picked Peggy up to show her the unicorn she'd shaped out of slime.

That gave Peggy a new idea! Maybe the unicorn slime could turn her into a unicorn. . . .

Wriggling out of Chloe's grasp, she dived headfirst into the slime, and rolled around and around in it. When her fur

was entirely coated in glittery slime, Peggy stood up. She still had paws, not hooves. And they were completely covered in sparkly slime!

"You need a bath, Peggy," said Chloe, laughing.

Peggy waited for Chloe to lick her clean with her tongue, but instead Chloe carried her into the bathroom and ran a bath. Chloe added two capfuls of strawberry-scented bath foam and gently set Peggy down in the warm, sudsy water.

"Good girl," said Chloe, scrubbing the slime off Peggy's fur.

Ooh, this is nice, thought Peggy.

When Peggy's fur was clean, Chloe lifted her out of the bath and wrapped her in a fluffy towel.

"All clean," she said, setting Peggy down in front of the mirror.

A wet dog with big brown eyes, a wrinkly face, and bubbles on her head stared back at Peggy. In spite of everything she had tried today, she was still just a pug.

"Look!" said Chloe, shaping the bubbles

on Peggy's head into a horn. "You're a pugicorn!"

Peggy's eyes widened in surprise. There was a beautiful white horn on her head! Clever Chloe had turned her into a unicorn! But then—

POP! POP! POP!

The bubbles burst. Along with Peggy's hopes of becoming a unicorn.

Chapter Six

The next day Chloe took Peggy to the park. She didn't get cross when Peggy spent ages snuffling in the crunchy dried leaves or barking at squirrels. She didn't mind throwing a tennis ball again and again for Peggy to retrieve. And when they met other children in the playground, Chloe waited patiently while they patted Peggy.

As they walked back home, they passed by the village hall. The doors were propped open and inside, people were busy painting a backdrop.

"It's the village nativity play tonight, Peggy," said Chloe.

Peggy looked up at her questioningly.

"I wanted to be an angel like Ruby, but I'm playing a stupid shepherd instead," grumbled Chloe.

Loud music could be heard coming from upstairs when they got back home. "We wish you a merry Christmas!" Finn sang, off-key.

Yikes, thought Peggy, her floppy black ears hurting as Finn screeched a high note.

Mum was in the kitchen, sewing a piece of brown fabric.

"What's that horrible sound?" asked Chloe, unclipping Peggy's lead.

"Finn's practicing for the nativity," said Mum. "His band is playing."

DING! A timer sounded and Dad took a tray of mince pies out of the oven.

"Those smell good," said Chloe, helping herself to one and breaking off a bit for Peggy.

"Don't eat them all," Dad said, smiling. "I'm bringing them to the show tonight."

Thirsty after her long walk, Peggy slurped up lots of water from her new red water bowl.

Mum handed Chloe the brown robe she'd been sewing. "Here's your shepherd costume. I hope it fits."

"I'll try it on later," Chloe said unenthusiastically.

Peggy followed Chloe into the living room. Tossing her costume onto the sofa, Chloe switched on the television. "Ruby!" she called. "*Sparkalina* is starting!"

As the theme tune began to play, Ruby ran into the living room wearing a white dress, a gold tinsel halo on her head, and gauzy wings on her back. She danced around the room, showing off her costume. "I be an angel."

Chloe and Peggy eyed Ruby's wings enviously. *Can Ruby's wings really make her fly?* wondered Peggy.

The girls settled on the sofa, and Peggy clambered up too, then curled up on the soft fabric of Chloe's shepherd costume.

Chloe stroked Peggy's fur as they watched television. In this episode, Sparkalina was teaching a fairy how to fly. The unicorn sang:

Just flap your wings if you want to fly,

Think happy thoughts and you'll reach

the sky.

That sounds easy, thought Peggy. All it took was happy thoughts. And wings, of course.

"I'd better try on my costume," said Chloe when the show finished. Gently pushing Peggy off the brown robe, she picked it up. There was a big wet patch where Peggy had been sitting.

"Oh no!" wailed Chloe. "Peggy peed on my shepherd costume!"

Oopsie!

Peggy hadn't even realized she had piddled! If dogs could blush, Peggy's tan-colored fur would have turned bright red. She'd been house-trained for weeks and hadn't had an accident for ages!

"Gross," said Finn, wrinkling his nose in disgust.

"This is the last thing I need right now," said Mum, looking exasperated.

They'll never let me

stay now, Peggy thought, her head bowed in shame.

"Puppies are only little," said Dad, squirting the sofa with cleaning spray. "They can't hold their wee in very long."

"Adopting a puppy is a big responsibility," said Mum. "You need to take them out more often than adult dogs."

"What are we going to do about my costume?" said Chloe.

"I can wash it," offered Dad.

"But it won't dry in time," said Chloe.

"I don't have time to sew a new one, so we'll just need to improvise," said Mum. Everyone hunted around the house for things to make a new costume.

"Here, Chloe," said Finn, handing her his dressing gown. "You can wear this."

"And this can go on your head," said Mum, draping a tea towel over Chloe's curly hair.

Dad tied garden twine around Chloe's waist like a belt, then put another bit around her head. "Ta-da! Now you're a shepherd."

But Chloe still looked glum. "Who's going to look after Peggy while we're at the show?"

Mum frowned. "Hmmm," she said. "I hadn't thought of that."

Peggy whined softly, hoping that they wouldn't leave her on her own.

"I know!" exclaimed Chloe. "If I'm a shepherd, Peggy can be my sheep! She just needs a costume."

Mum found a fleecy white cardigan that Ruby had outgrown. She cut off the sleeves and put Peggy's front legs through the armholes. It fit perfectly! Chloe made ears out of black card and cotton balls and glued them to a soft headband. Then she tied a little bell onto Peggy's collar.

Tucking Peggy into the crook of her arm, Chloe grinned. "This is even better than being an angel!"

They drove to the village hall. Dad helped Finn set up his drum kit at the side of the stage, where Jasmine and the band were tuning up their instruments. Chloe and

Ruby joined the rest of the cast backstage. Everyone crowded around to stroke Peggy.

"I wish I was a shepherd," said an innkeeper holding a lantern.

"I should have made a camel costume for my dog," said a king in a fancy gold-and-purple costume.

"Your dog is sooooo cute," said the little girl playing Mary, who was holding a baby doll wrapped in a blanket.

"I know," Chloe said proudly, adjusting Peggy's sheep ears.

When the play was about to begin, Ruby tugged on Chloe's sleeve. "I scared," she whispered.

"I thought you wanted to be an angel?" Chloe whispered back.

Ruby shook her head, her eyes wide with fright. She wriggled out of her angel wings and dropped them by the side of the stage.

"Go and sit with Mum and Dad," whispered Chloe. She pulled back the stage curtains, and Ruby ran to join her parents in the audience.

The play began with Mary and Joseph wheeling a cardboard donkey mounted on a skateboard onto the stage. Peggy's fur prickled with excitement as she and Chloe waited in the wings. Finally it was time for the shepherds to make their entrance.

"Aww!" cooed the audience as Peggy waddled onto the stage behind Chloe.

AAARROOO! AAAROOO! Peggy howled along as the shepherds sang "Away in a Manger."

As the three kings came onstage, Peggy suddenly spotted Ruby's angel wings by the

side of the stage. *Maybe those can help me fly like Sparkalina!* She darted over to the wings and bit them. Now it was time to fly!

As she held the wings in her mouth, she remembered what Sparkalina had told the fairy, and filled her head with happy thoughts.

Falling asleep next to Chloe . . .

Playing fetch with Ruby . . .

Getting a pat from Dad . . .

Here goes . . . , she thought. She raced to the edge of the stage as the cast launched into their final carol.

"Peggy, no!" cried Chloe, reaching out with her shepherd's crook to try to catch her. But Chloe wasn't fast enough.

Squeezing her eyes shut, Peggy jumped off the stage.

WHEE! For one wonderful moment she was flying, but then—

CRASH! CLANG! BANG!

She landed on Finn's drum kit.

Cymbals clattered to the ground. A bass

drum rolled away. Music stands toppled over.

Oh no, thought Peggy. *Finn's really going to hate me now.* Her bottom was sore, but that wasn't what hurt most of all. She'd ruined the show.

As someone picked her up gently, Peggy raised her eyes in dread, expecting to see an angry face. But Finn was smiling!

"Woo-hoo!" he cheered. "Now THAT'S what I call a drum solo!"

Now the whole audience was clapping! Finn passed Peggy up to Chloe, so the dog could take a bow with the rest of the cast.

Afterward, they all celebrated with hot chocolate and Dad's mince pies.

"Best. Nativity. Play. Ever," said Finn.

"And all because of Peggy," said Mum. "Ruby didn't want to be an angel—but Peggy did."

"I told you she was a star," said Chloe, beaming.

But I don't want to be an angel OR a star, thought Peggy. *I want to be a unicorn.* And with Christmas Eve only a day away, time was running out to convince Chloe's family to let her stay. She HAD to stop messing things up!

Chapter Seven

"Wake up, sleepyhead!" Chloe said, shaking Peggy awake the morning before Christmas. Peggy burrowed deeper into the duvet, too warm and comfy to move.

"Seriously, you've got to see this," said Chloe. She picked Peggy up and carried her to the window.

Peggy pressed her nose against the chilly windowpane. She blinked in confusion. The grass was covered in a blanket of white that sparkled like diamonds in the early-morning sunshine.

"It snowed!" said Chloe.

Now wide awake, Peggy let out a yip. She wasn't sure what snow was, but Chloe's excitement was contagious.

Chloe charged downstairs and grabbed her coat, hat, and boots.

"Not so fast," said Dad, who was waxing an old wooden sled with curved runners. "You need to eat some breakfast first."

Sighing impatiently, Chloe sat down at the table. Finn was tucking into a plate of scrambled eggs, while Ruby was eating porridge in her high chair. Peggy licked up a blob of porridge that had fallen onto the floor.

"Where did you get that sled, Dad?" asked Chloe.

"It was in the loft," said Dad. "My granddad made it for me when I was a little boy."

"It's so exciting!" said Mum, sipping her coffee. "We haven't had a white Christmas in years."

Peggy had a few bites of food, and then she danced around at the back door.

"Peggy needs a wee," said Chloe, scooping up her last bite of porridge. "Can I go out now?"

"As long as you bundle up," said Mum.

Chloe got dressed, then helped Ruby zip up her coat and put on her boots. Then they pulled on woolly hats and mittens. Finn got ready too, and seemed almost as excited about the snow as his younger sisters.

"What about Peggy?" worried Chloe. "Won't she be cold?"

"She'll be fine," said Dad. "Her fur will keep her warm."

Chloe opened the back door. A blast of cold air rushed in, hitting Peggy in the face. Chloe, Ruby, and Finn ran outside, their boots leaving holes in the snow. But Peggy hesitated in the doorway.

"Come on, Peggy," coaxed Chloe. "Don't be scared. Snow is fun."

Peggy knew she could trust Chloe.

Gingerly, she stepped outside, her paws sinking into the snow.

Whoa! She hadn't expected it to be so cold. The snow made her paws feel numb. Peggy stuck out her tongue and lapped at the snow. *Hmm*, she thought, as the snow melted in her mouth. *That's interesting.* To her surprise, snow tasted exactly like water!

Ruby scooped up a handful of snow and licked it.

"Whatever you do, don't eat the yellow snow," joked Finn, pointing at the puddle Peggy had left in the snow.

The snow was so deep, it reached the top of Peggy's head! Her furry little body made tunnels in the snow as she explored the garden.

WHOOSH! A snowball whistled through the air and—*PLOP!*—hit Chloe on the back.

"Bullseye!" laughed Finn.

"You asked for it!" cried Chloe, quickly making a snowball and firing it back at her brother. Then Ruby threw one at him too.

"Hey! Two against one isn't fair," cried Finn, ducking.

Soon a snowball fight was in full swing. The children ran around the garden, ducking behind trees and jumping out to pelt each other with snowballs.

WOOF! WOOF! WOOF! Peggy bounded through the drifts of snow, barking gleefully as snowballs whizzed through the air. SPLAT! A snowball landed on Peggy's head.

"Oops! Sorry, Peggy," said Finn, brushing snow off the pug's fur. "I was aiming for Chloe."

"Time out!" gasped Chloe, collapsing on her back in the snow. "I need to catch my breath." She fanned her arms and legs out to the sides, making an angel shape in the snow. Ruby copied her, brushing her arms up and down.

"Let's make a snowman," suggested Finn.

"I've got a better idea!" said Chloe. "Let's make a snow unicorn!"

"Yes!" cried Ruby, scrambling to her feet. "Noonicorn!"

Finn pulled a face. "Unicorns are lame."

"No they aren't," said Chloe. "They're really cool. They can do magic."

Finn rolled his eyes, but he helped his sisters build a snow unicorn. As Peggy snuffled around in the snow, the three children formed the shape of a horse, patting it down with their mittens.

"I know!" cried Chloe. She broke off a big icicle hanging from the windowsill and stuck it on the unicorn's head. "Now it's got a horn!"

Peggy stared at the snow unicorn

thoughtfully. Maybe she could get a unicorn horn, too. . . .

She plowed through the snow to a bush with icicles dripping from it. She prodded the icicle with her head. *SNAP!* The icicle broke off and landed on her paw—pointy side down!

Ouch!

Finn's phone beeped and he pulled it out of his pocket. "Jasmine says we should come to the park," he said, reading his message.

Finn pulled Ruby on the sled, while Chloe and Peggy trudged along the snowy sidewalk. In the park, children were whizzing down a hill on plastic sleds and inflatable rings. One kid was even sliding down on a tea tray!

As Finn chatted to Jasmine, Ruby sat on Dad's wooden sled.

"Ready?" Chloe asked her sister.

Ruby shook her head. "I scared."

"Okay, I'll come with you," said Chloe. She sat behind Ruby on the sled. "Back in a second, Peggy." Then—*WHOOSH!*—the girls slid down the hill, squealing in delight.

As she waited for the girls to return, a flash of red caught Peggy's eye. It was a cardinal hopping along, its glossy red feathers bright against the white snow. "Hey!" Peggy barked. "Can you teach me how to fly?"

Startled, the cardinal flapped its wings and flew into the air.

"Wait!" barked Peggy, chasing after the bird. "I just want to talk to you!" She bounded after the cardinal, until she couldn't see it anymore. Then, peeking over the top of the snow, she suddenly realized she couldn't see anyone.

Don't panic, Peggy told herself. *Just go back*

the way you came. But her pawprints were muddled up with all the other tracks in the snow. She ran this way and that way— trying to find her way back to Chloe—but only got more and more lost.

Peggy shivered. *Where is everyone?* What if she never found her way back? She'd freeze out here in the cold!

Peggy started to run, but her paws slipped out from under her. She tried to stop, but she couldn't grip the slippery snow.

Faster and faster she slid, whooshing down the hill until—

THUMP!—she crashed into an enormous snowbank at the bottom!

Peggy scrubbed her face with a paw, wiping snow out of her eyes. "Help!" she yelped, trying to wriggle out of the snowbank. Her paws scrabbled around, but it was no use—she was stuck!

Peggy barked and barked, but cries of delight from children sledding down the

hill drowned out her pitiful yelps. She craned her neck, panicking as she tried to peer over the top of the snow.

"HELP!" she howled desperately, her nose feeling numb and her paws icy cold.

"Peggy!" cried a familiar voice.

Chloe dug Peggy out of the snow and hugged her tight. "Oh, Peggy!" she cried.

"I was so worried! You poor thing!"

Finn pulled the girls home on the sled, with Peggy tucked into Chloe's coat.

At home, Chloe wrapped Peggy in a blanket. They cuddled together on the sofa and watched the *Sparkalina* Christmas special. Peggy felt safe and contented. She wished she could live with the girls for ever.

After dinner, Chloe arranged some mince pies on a plate. "These are for Santa."

"Don't forget Rudolph," said Finn, getting carrots out of the refrigerator.

They set the treats on a table near the Christmas tree. Then Chloe took out a piece of paper and started to write.

"What are you doing?" Finn asked his sister.

"Writing a note to Santa," explained Chloe.

"What does it say?" Finn asked curiously, trying to read over her shoulder. Peggy was wondering the same thing herself.

"None of your business," said Chloe, covering up the words. "It's secret."

Peggy didn't know how to read, but she could guess what the note said. Chloe was reminding Santa about what she wanted most of all—a unicorn.

Peggy gazed out of the window sadly. The snow unicorn the children had made

glowed in the moonlight. Its icicle horn reflected the colors of the outdoor fairy lights, twinkling red, green, blue, and yellow. *When Sparkalina's horn glows, it can do magic*, thought Peggy. Maybe this unicorn could do magic too?

It was worth a try. Tomorrow was Christmas Day. This was Peggy's last chance. If she failed, she'd be going back to the dog shelter once the Christmas holidays were over.

Please will you turn me into a unicorn? she begged the snow unicorn, wishing with all her heart. *So that I can make Chloe happy and stay with her family forever?*

Chapter Eight

It was still dark when Peggy felt Chloe stir on Christmas morning. Chloe slid out of bed, wearing her new starry unicorn pajamas.

Peggy whined sleepily, not wanting Chloe to go.

"Sssh!" Chloe whispered, pressing a finger

to her lips. "It's still really early."

Chloe tiptoed out of her bedroom and down the stairs, with Peggy padding along behind her.

In the dark living room, an amazing sight met Peggy's eyes. The Christmas tree's lights were twinkling, lighting up piles of presents wrapped in beautiful paper and topped with shiny bows and ribbons.

"Santa came!" squealed Chloe. "This one's for me!" she cried, rooting around underneath the tree and dragging out a big present with her name on it. She ripped off the wrapping paper. "Oh, wow!" she cried, holding up a Sparkalina toy. It had a

light-up horn and wings that really flapped. "It's just what I wanted!"

But Peggy's Christmas wish hadn't come true—she was still a pug. It didn't even matter because Chloe had gotten a unicorn from Santa and didn't need another one. Peggy swallowed her disappointment. She didn't want anything to spoil what little time she had left with Chloe and her family.

To console herself, Peggy licked up the crumbs on the plate that had held the mince pies for Santa.

By now, the sun was starting to rise and the rest of the family made their way sleepily downstairs, yawning and rubbing their eyes.

"Happy Christmas," said Mum. She hugged each of the children, then gave Peggy a cuddle.

"Pwesents!" squealed Ruby, running over to the fireplace. Hanging from the mantel was a stocking with each child's name on it.

"Santa even brought one for Peggy!" said Chloe. She took the stocking down and showed it to Peggy. It was bulging with dog

treats and a chew toy shaped like a candy cane.

"Of course he did," said Finn. "He always brought one for Baxter, too."

Peggy glanced at Chloe anxiously, worried that the mention of her old dog would upset her. But Chloe smiled. "Yeah," she said, chuckling. "But Baxter was always more interested in the Christmas turkey."

"Ooh! That reminds me," said Mum. "I'd better go and put the turkey in the oven." She hurried into the kitchen.

The children were too excited to eat breakfast. Everyone took turns opening presents, as Peggy rolled around in the

discarded wrapping paper. She loved the crinkly noise it made under her paws!

"Oh, it's beautiful!" said Mum, unwrapping a macaroni necklace that Ruby had made at nursery school.

"Wicked!" said Finn, opening up a new soccer game for his console.

Soon, all the presents had been opened and the delicious smell of roasting turkey wafted through the air. Dad was helping Ruby assemble her new doll's house. Mum was munching chocolates and reading the book Chloe had bought her. Finn was throwing balls of wrapping paper for Peggy to fetch.

Only Chloe didn't seem happy as she brushed her toy unicorn's mane listlessly.

"What's wrong?" asked Mum, putting her arm around Chloe. "Don't you like your presents?"

Chloe nodded and smiled weakly. "No, I love them."

Peggy's heart felt like it was breaking. She suddenly realized why Chloe was disappointed. Santa hadn't granted her secret wish. He hadn't brought her a *real* unicorn.

"Oh, look," said Dad, reaching behind the Christmas tree. "There's still one more present back here. We must have missed it."

"Who's it for?" asked Chloe.

"Peggy," said Dad, studying the label. "But it doesn't say who it's from."

Chloe helped Peggy unwrap the box. She lifted off the lid and took out something soft and white. It had little rainbow-colored wings and a shiny horn attached to the hood. It was a tiny unicorn onesie!

"That is so cute!" cried Chloe. She quickly put Peggy's paws into the sleeves and pulled the hood over Peggy's head. "She looks adorable!"

"Peggy's a pugicorn!" said Finn.

Everyone laughed. But then Chloe's face fell. "They probably won't let her wear it at the dog shelter," she said sadly.

"She can wear it whenever she likes," said Mum.

Dad nodded. "This is her home now."

Chloe stared at her parents in disbelief. "You mean—"

"We all love Peggy," said Mum.

"Even Finn?" asked Chloe.

Her brother smiled. "She's actually pretty cool for a little dog."

"So we've decided to adopt her," said Mum.

"We couldn't imagine taking her back to the dog shelter," said Dad. "Peggy's part of the family now."

"So Santa *did* grant my Christmas wish," said Chloe with a grin. "I told him that more than anything else, I wanted Peggy to live with us forever."

Peggy couldn't believe what she was hearing. Was this really her forever home? She'd been so sure Chloe wanted a unicorn, when really Chloe had wanted *her* all along.

"Yay!" cheered Ruby. She picked Peggy up and cuddled her tight.

Gah! thought Peggy, struggling to breathe.

"Don't strangle her," said Chloe, extracting Peggy from her little sister's over-enthusiastic embrace.

"I'm going to tell Jasmine the good news," said Finn, grinning as he tapped a message on his phone.

Chloe held Peggy up to the window so she could see her new outfit in the reflection. Even with her onesie on, Peggy looked like a pug. But she knew it didn't matter. She didn't need to be a unicorn for her dreams to come true. She just needed to be herself.

Across the lawn, Peggy saw the snow unicorn, its icicle horn beginning to melt in the sunshine. She wasn't sure who had granted her Christmas wish. It might have been Santa. It might have been the snow unicorn. She'd never know. But whoever it was had made her the happiest puppy in the world. "Thank you!" she barked joyfully.

"Happy Christmas, Peggy," said Chloe, cuddling her tight.

Peggy licked Chloe's face. Peggy's mum had been right, after all—there *was* a perfect owner for every dog. And Peggy had finally found hers.

Read on for a sneak peek at
The Pug Who Wanted
to Be a Reindeer

Peggy the pug's flat, black nose twitched as she napped on the sofa. As carols played softly on the radio and the spicy scent of gingerbread wafted from the kitchen, Peggy dreamed about Christmas. It was her favorite time of year—because it was in

December last year that she'd found her home.

The sound of the front door opening jolted Peggy awake.

"We're home!" cried a voice from the hallway, followed by the thud of backpacks dropping to the floor.

Chloe! thought Peggy, scrambling to her feet. Curly little tail wagging, she raced out to the hallway as fast as her short legs could carry her.

"Hi, Peggy!" cried Chloe, a dark-haired girl wrapped up in a coat and a woolly scarf. She crouched down on the floor to stroke Peggy's tan-colored fur.

"I miss you *sooooooo* much when you're at school!" Peggy told her best friend.